Nate The Great
and The
Lost List

Nate the Great
and The
Lost List

by Marjorie Weinman Sharmat

illustrations by Marc Simont

A Yearling Book

Published by Yearling, an imprint of Random House Children's Books
a division of Random House, Inc., New York

Visit us on the Web! www.randomhouse.com/kids

Educators and librarians, for a variety of teaching tools, visit us at
www.randomhouse.com/teachers

ISBN: 978-0-440-46282-8

Reprinted by arrangement with The Putnam Publishing Group Inc.
Printed in the United States of America
May 2007
49 48 47

For someone special,
my cousin Rhoda

I, Nate the Great,
am a busy detective.
One morning I was not busy.
I was on my vacation.
I was sitting under a tree
enjoying the breeze
with my dog, Sludge,
and a pancake.
He needed a vacation too.
My friend Claude

came into the yard.

I knew that he

had lost something.

Claude was always losing things.

"I lost my way to your house,"

he said. "And then I found it."

"What else did you lose?"

"I lost the grocery list

I was taking to the store.

Can you help me find it?"

"I, Nate the Great,

am on my vacation," I said.

"When will your vacation be over?"

"At lunch."

"I need the list before lunch,"
Claude said.

"Very well. I, Nate the Great,
will take your case.
Tell me, what was on the list?"

"If I could remember, I wouldn't
need the list," Claude said.

"Good thinking," I said.

"Does anyone know what
was on the list?"

"My father," Claude said.

"He wrote it."

"Good. Can you find your father?"

"No, he won't be home
until lunch."

"Can you remember
some of the list?"

"Yes," Claude said. "I remember
salt, milk, butter, flour,
sugar, and tuna fish."

"Now, tell me, where did you
lose the list?"

"If I knew, I could
find it," Claude said.

"You can't be sure
of that," I said.

"What streets did you walk on?"

"I'm not sure," Claude said.

"I lost my way a few times."

"Then I, Nate the Great,
know what to do.
I will draw a map
of every street
between your house
and the grocery store
and we will follow the map."
Sludge and I got up.
Our vacation was over.

I got two pieces of paper
and a pen.
I drew a map
on one piece of paper.

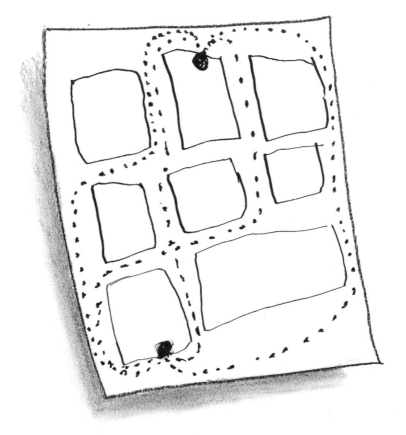

I wrote on the other:

Dear Mother,
Something is
lost. When I find
it, I will be back.
Love,
Nate the Great

Claude said,

"I will walk with you."

"Don't get lost," I said,

"or I will have

two cases to solve."

We walked between Claude's house

and the grocery store

and then between the grocery store

and Claude's house.

Sludge sniffed.

But we could not find the list.

"Perhaps it blew away," I said.

I dropped the map

on the ground.

"What are you doing?"

Claude asked.

"I am dropping the map.

Whichever direction it goes

will show us the way

the wind is blowing.

Perhaps your list blew

in the same direction."

The map blew toward Rosamond's
house and disappeared.
"I will go
to Rosamond's house," I said.
"I will ask her if
she has seen your list."

"I will go to my house
and wait," Claude said.
"We are in front
of your house," I said.
"Yes, that makes it
easy to find," Claude said.

Sludge and I went
to Rosamond's house.
Rosamond opened the door.
Rosamond is a very strange girl.
Today she looked
more than strange.
She looked strange and white.
She was covered with flour.
Sludge sniffed hard.
I sniffed hard.
Rosamond smelled terrific.
Pancakes!
She was making pancakes.
We walked in.
Rosamond's four black cats
were there.

Today they were white, too.

The cats looked at Sludge.

They were not afraid of him.

Nobody is afraid of Sludge.

"I am making cat pancakes

for my cats," Rosamond said,

"from a new recipe."

"I would like to taste

cat pancakes," I said.

"You are not a cat," Rosamond said.

"I would like to

taste them anyway," I said.

"A pancake is a pancake."

Rosamond and I sat down.

I ate a pancake.

It tasted fishy.

I ate another.

It tasted fishier.

"I am looking for Claude's
grocery list," I said.
"I think the wind blew it
toward your house.
Have you seen it?"
"I haven't seen a grocery list,"
Rosamond said. "But—"
"But what?"
"But I see Annie

and her dog, Fang,
outside my window, and—"
"And what?"
"And Fang has a piece of
paper in his mouth.
It might be the grocery list."

I got up.

"Thank you for your help
and your pancakes," I said.

"I am having a cat pancake party
this morning," Rosamond said.

"I have invited
all the cats I know.

Can you come?"

"I am not a cat," I said.

"That's what I told
you before," Rosamond said.
Sludge and I went out
to talk to Annie and Fang.
I like Annie.
I try to like Fang.
"Hello," I said. "I am looking
for Claude's grocery list,
and I think Fang has found it.

It's between his teeth."

"He won't let
that paper go," Annie said.

"Can you pull it out?" I asked.

"No," Annie said.

"Fang would get mad."

"I would not like to see
Fang mad," I said.

"I, Nate the Great, say
that we should keep anybody
with sharp teeth happy.
Very happy."

I had a problem.

How could I get the paper
out of Fang's mouth?

Suddenly I had the answer.

"Sludge," I said. "Bark!"

Sludge barked.

Sludge barks funny.

But that does not matter.

Fang barked back.

The piece of paper

dropped from his mouth.

I reached for it.

But the wind blew it
down the street.
I went after it.
Sludge went after me.
Fang went after Sludge.

Annie went after Fang.

The paper went around the corner.

I went around the corner.

Sludge went around the corner.

Fang went around the corner.

Annie went around the corner.

The paper blew
into a fence.

I grabbed the paper.

The case was almost over.

I looked at the paper.

I saw many lines.

The paper was my map.

"The list is still lost," I said.

"I need more clues."

I thanked Annie and Fang

for their help.

Sludge and I

walked to Claude's house.

Claude was home.

He was not lost.

It was a good sign.

"I, Nate the Great, have not

found your list," I said.

"Can you remember anything else

that was written on it?"

"How will that help

you find it?" Claude asked.

"Trust me," I said.

"I remember! I remember
two more things," Claude said.
"Eggs and baking powder."
"Very good," I said.
"Can you find the list
before lunch?" Claude asked.
"I hope so," I said.

"Come to my house at eleven."
Sludge and I walked home slowly.
This was a hard case. At home
I made myself some pancakes.
I mixed eggs, flour, salt,
baking powder, milk, butter,
and sugar together and cooked them.

I gave Sludge a bone.

I ate and thought.

I thought about the grocery list.

I thought about Rosamond
and her fishy cat pancakes.

I thought about Annie and Fang
and the map.

I put ideas together.

I took them apart.

Then I had a big idea.

I knew I must go back to
Rosamond's house.

I did not want to do that.

I did not want to be
at a party with Rosamond
and all the cats she knew.

But I had a job to do.

I had a case to solve.

Sludge and I walked quickly to

Rosamond's house.

I said hello to Rosamond
and more cats
than I could count.
They were all over
Rosamond's floor,

Rosamond's tables,

Rosamond's chairs,

and Rosamond.

"I came to talk about

your cat pancakes," I said.

"Would you like more?"

Rosamond asked.

"I would like to see

your recipe," I said.

"Here it is," Rosamond said.

"There are no directions

in this recipe," I said.

"I don't need any," Rosamond said.

"I just mix

some of everything together."

"Tell me, where did you

get this recipe?"

"I found it today," Rosamond said.

"Aha! You found it," I said.

"Did you find it

near your house?"

"Yes," Rosamond said.

"How did you know that?"

"I have something to tell you.

I, Nate the Great, say that
your cat pancake recipe
is Claude's grocery list."
I stood tall.
I cleared my throat.
I read the recipe.
"Salt
milk
butter
flour
tuna fish
eggs
baking powder
sugar
salmon
liver."

"Oh," Rosamond said.
"When I found the paper,
I thought it was a
cat pancake recipe."

"Yes," I said. "And when I
saw Fang holding a piece of paper,
I thought it was a grocery list.
I thought it was what I
hoped it was.

When you saw the grocery list,
you thought it was
what you hoped it was.
A cat pancake recipe.

I, Nate the Great, thought of that
when I was making pancakes.
I mixed eggs, flour, salt,
baking powder, milk, butter,
and sugar.
Claude had told me they
were on his list.
The other thing he remembered
on the list was tuna fish.
Cats like tuna fish.
So—cat pancakes!"

"Oh," Rosamond said.
"Well, Claude
can have his paper back.
I will keep the recipe
in my head."
"That is a good place for it,"
I said. "It cannot blow away."
I said good-bye to Rosamond
and more cats
than I could count.

Sludge and I went home
with the list.
The case was solved.
And it was almost eleven o'clock.
When Claude comes at eleven,
I will give him his list.

It is now past eleven o'clock.

It is now past eleven-thirty.

Claude has not shown up.

I do not see him anywhere.

I hope Claude has not lost
himself.

It is now past twelve.

Here comes Claude.

I am glad I do not have
to look for him.

I am glad the case is over.

I, Nate the Great,

have something important to do.

I, Nate the Great,

am going to finish

my vacation.

~Extra~
Fun Activities!

What's Inside

How did Oliver lose his list?
The wind blew it away.
Nate wanted to know more.
He went to the library.
Here's what he found.

NATE'S NOTES: Wind

Wind is moving air. It spreads the sun's heat around the earth.

Wind is invisible, but its effects are not. You can "see" the wind by watching trees sway or flags flutter.

Wind can be gentle (a breeze).

Wind can be fierce (a hurricane).

Wind can make energy by turning windmills.

Winds as gentle as 13 miles per hour will "ground" mosquitoes. That means they can't fly. Bring on the wind!

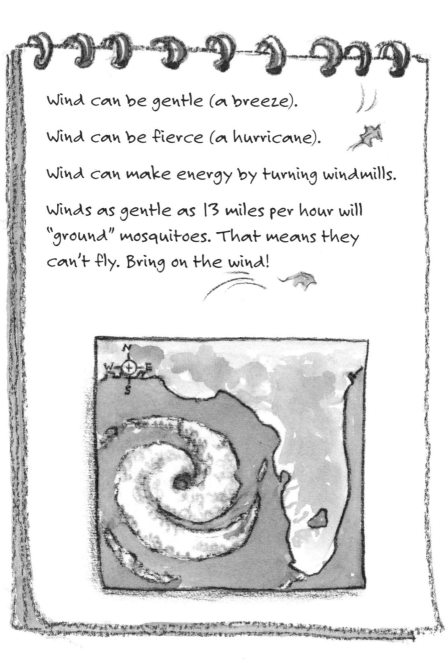

How to Make a Pinwheel

*Pinwheels are fun! Make one and
learn more about how the wind works.*

Ask an adult to help you with this.

GET TOGETHER:

- a square piece of construction paper
- a new, unsharpened pencil with an eraser
- a ruler
- a straight pin
- scissors

MAKE YOUR PINWHEEL:

1. Lay the paper on a table. Use the pencil
   and the ruler to draw a line diagonally
   from each corner to the opposite one.
   When you're finished, the paper should
   look like this:

2. Use the pin to punch a small hole where the two lines cross.
3. Starting at the outer edge, cut along each line. Stop about an inch from the center hole. You can look at your ruler to see how long an inch is.
4. You now have four flaps. Use the pin to poke a hole in the top left corner of the top flap. Turn the paper so that a new flap is on top. Again, poke a hole in the top left corner. Repeat two more times, so that each flap has a hole in it.

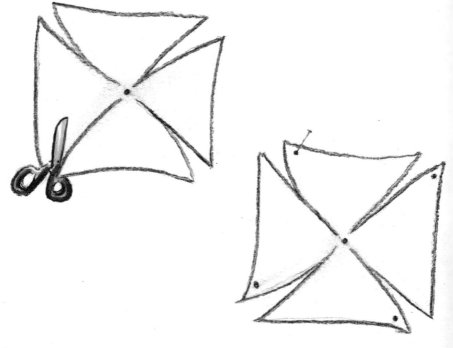

5. Pick up a flap at a punched corner. Carefully curl it toward the center hole. Slide the pin through the hole in the flap. Be sure not to poke yourself! Repeat with the other three flaps.
6. Now push the pin through the center hole. Your pinwheel should look like this one.
7. Lay the pencil on the table. Carefully push the pin into the eraser.
8. Hold the pinwheel by the pencil. Play with your pinwheel in the wind!

NATE'S NOTES: Maps

Nate likes maps. They're flat, easy to carry, and useful. He found some information about maps in the encyclopedia.

A MAP is a flat picture of all or part of the earth's surface. A GLOBE is a map drawn on a sphere (or ball). A CHART is a map used to navigate the ocean or another waterway.

A grid system makes a map easier to read. LONGITUDE lines run from north to south. LATITUDE lines run from east to west. The scale of a map shows how much smaller it is than the areas on the earth it depicts. An ARROW, or COMPASS, often shows you which way is north.

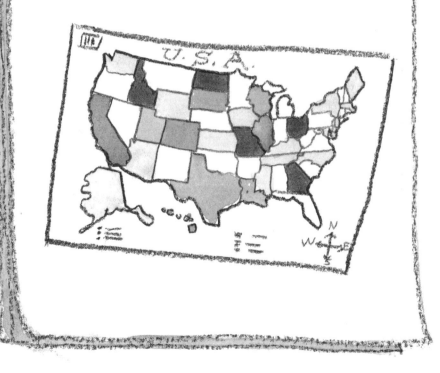

People also make globes and maps of the moon and the stars. It's harder to create a simple map of the sun, the moon, or the other planets because their positions change every day.

The oldest map in the world may be a small clay tablet about 4,000 years old. It shows part of a land called Mesopotamia. The area shown is now Iraq.

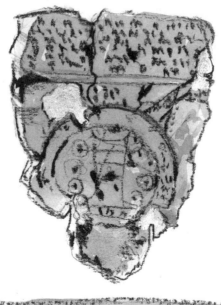

The first map of North America may be the "Vinland Map." Some experts date it to the year 1434. That's nearly sixty years before Columbus sailed to America. It probably shows part of what is now eastern Canada. Experts say Viking explorers drew the map. They called the area Vinland because of the grapevines they found growing there. Other experts consider this map a fake!

Google Earth is a really cool new kind of map. It lets you use your computer to "fly over" any location on earth. Get started at www.earth.google.com.

How to Make Cat Pancakes

Rosamond made pancakes for her cats to eat. Rosamond is weird. Pancakes are for people. If you really like cats, make these cat-shaped pancakes. But feed them to your friends, your family, and, of course, yourself.

Ask an adult to help you with this recipe.

GET TOGETHER:

- a mixing bowl
- 1 cup of flour
- a pinch of salt
- 2 tablespoons of sugar
- $1\frac{1}{2}$ teaspoons of baking powder
- 1 egg
- 2 tablespoons of melted butter
- $1\frac{1}{2}$ cups of milk
- a nonstick skillet
- cat-shaped cookie cutters
- syrup

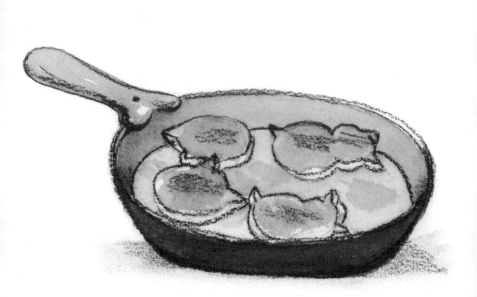

MAKE YOUR CAT PANCAKES:

1. In the bowl, mix together the flour, salt, sugar, and baking powder.
2. Add the egg, melted butter, and milk. Stir until just mixed together. Lumps are okay.
3. Warm the skillet over medium heat. Drop a tiny bit of water on the skillet. If the water skitters around, the skillet is hot enough.

4. For each pancake, pour about half a cup of batter onto the skillet. Wait until your pancakes have bubbles on top. Flip them. Cook them one more minute.
5. Put your pancakes on a plate. Use the cookie cutter to cut each pancake into one or more cat shapes.
6. Serve your pancakes with syrup on top.

Pancake trimmings make a good snack for a hungry dog.

Funny Pages

Q: What do cats eat for breakfast?
A: *Mice Krispies!*

Q: What do you call a cat who eats lemons?
A: *A sourpuss!*

Q: What do Italian cats like for dinner?
A: *Spa-catti!*

Q: What happened when the cat ate the comedian?
A: *He felt funny!*

Q: What does Rosamond feed her cats on a hot day?
A: *Mice cream cones!*

Q: What is Super Hex's favorite color?
A: *Purrple!*

How to Improve Your Memory

A detective needs a good memory. It helps the detective keep track of clues, or find the way home. Oliver could improve his memory with these tips. That is, if he could remember to use them.

Tip 1: *Pay attention to one thing at a time.* It's hard to remember anything if you are thinking about two things at once. That's why Nate usually takes only one case at a time!

Tip 2: *Get it right the first time.* "Unlearning" wrong information is more difficult than learning new information. So slow down and get your facts straight.

Tip 3: *Create a picture in your mind.*
To connect two facts you are trying to remember, make up a mental image. Make the picture silly if you can. Silly is easy to remember.

Say you are trying to remember that your cousin's birthday is November 10. You could imagine your cousin sitting down to Thanksgiving dinner—and eating ten turkeys! Thanksgiving helps you remember the month. The ten helps you recall the day.

Tip 4: *Create a story.*

Let's say you need to remember a short list, like a grocery list. Make up a story that includes all the items. Again, silliness works best. If your list includes salmon, red food coloring, and eggs, you might imagine a salmon swimming upstream to lay her eggs. But the salmon seems to be having a hard time. She pushes until she turns red in the face. Suddenly, out pops an egg! But it's not a salmon egg. It's a hen's egg! Test yourself. What were the three items on your list? That's right—salmon, red food coloring, and eggs.

Tip 5: *Use acrostics to remember how to spell words.* Take each letter of a hard-to-spell word. Assign a word to each one. Maybe you have a hard time remembering how to spell *beautiful.* See if it's easier to remember this phrase: "Beagles Eat Apples Under Tents IF U Leave."

Experts say cats have longer memories than dogs.
Cats can remember things for about 16 hours.
Dogs can only remember for about 5 minutes!

More Funny Pages

Doctor, Doctor, I've lost my memory!
When did this happen?
When did what happen?

Q: What did Annie's dog say to the vet who cured his memory loss?
A: *Fangs for the memories!*

Q: Why doesn't Oliver have a photographic memory?
A: *He doesn't have any film!*

Q: How are maps like fish?
A: *They both have scales!*

Q: Why don't maps ever win at cards?
A: *Because they always fold!*

Q: What game do people play at the grocery store?
A: *Price-tag!*

Q: What do bulls do when they go grocery shopping?
A: *They charge!*

Q: What color is the wind?
A: *Blew!*

Knock, knock.
Who's there?
Wendy.
Wendy who?
Wendy wind blows,
the cradle will rock.

Q: What did the book do
when a cold wind blew?
A: *Put on a book jacket!*

Have you helped solve all Nate the Great's mysteries?

❑ **Nate the Great**: Meet Nate, the great detective, and join him as he uses incredible sleuthing skills to solve his first big case.

❑ **Nate the Great Goes Undercover**: Who—or what—is raiding Oliver's trash every night? Nate bravely hides out in his friend's garbage can to catch the smelly crook.

❑ **Nate the Great and the Lost List**: Nate loves pancakes, but who ever heard of cats eating them? Is a strange recipe at the heart of this mystery?

❑ **Nate the Great and the Phony Clue**: Against ferocious cats, hostile adversaries, and a sly phony clue, Nate struggles to prove that he's still the world's greatest detective.

❑ **Nate the Great and the Sticky Case**: Nate is stuck with his stickiest case yet as he hunts for his friend Claude's valuable stegosaurus stamp.

❑ **Nate the Great and the Missing Key**: Nate isn't afraid to look anywhere—even under the nose of his friend's ferocious dog, Fang—to solve the case of the missing key.

❑ **Nate the Great and the Snowy Trail**: Nate has his work cut out for him when his friend Rosamond loses the birthday present she was going to give him. How can he find the present when Rosamond won't even tell him what it is?

❑ **Nate the Great and the Fishy Prize**: The trophy for the Smartest Pet Contest has disappeared! Will Sludge, Nate's clue-sniffing dog, help solve the case and prove he's worthy of the prize?

❑ **Nate the Great Stalks Stupidweed**: When his friend Oliver loses his special plant, Nate searches high and low. Who knew a little weed could be so tricky?

❑ **Nate the Great and the Boring Beach Bag**: It's no relaxing day at the beach for Nate and his trusty dog, Sludge, as they search through sand and surf for signs of a missing beach bag.

❑ **Nate the Great Goes Down in the Dumps**: Nate discovers that the only way to clean up this case is to visit the town dump. Detective work can sure get dirty!

❑ **Nate the Great and the Halloween Hunt**: It's Halloween, but Nate isn't trick-or-treating for candy. Can any of the witches, pirates, and robots he meets help him find a missing cat?

❑ **Nate the Great and the Musical Note**: Nate is used to looking for clues, not listening for them! When he gets caught in the middle of a musical riddle, can he hear his way out?

❑ **Nate the Great and the Stolen Base**: It's not easy to track down a stolen base, and Nate's hunt leads him to some strange places before he finds himself at bat once more.

❑ **Nate the Great and the Pillowcase**: When a pillowcase goes missing, Nate must venture into the dead of night to search for clues. Everyone sleeps easier knowing Nate the Great is on the case!

❑ **Nate the Great and the Mushy Valentine**: Nate hates mushy stuff. But when someone leaves a big heart taped to Sludge's doghouse, Nate must help his favorite pooch discover his secret admirer.

❑ **Nate the Great and the Tardy Tortoise**: Where did the mysterious green tortoise in Nate's yard come from? Nate needs all his patience to follow this slow . . . slow . . . clue.

❑ **Nate the Great and the Crunchy Christmas**: It's Christmas, and Fang, Annie's scary dog, is not feeling jolly. Can Nate find Fang's crunchy Christmas mail before Fang crunches on *him*?

❑ **Nate the Great Saves the King of Sweden**: Can Nate solve his *first-ever* international case without leaving his own neighborhood?

❑ **Nate the Great and Me: The Case of the Fleeing Fang**: A surprise Happy Detective Day party is great fun for Nate until his friend's dog disappears! Help Nate track down the missing pooch, and learn all the tricks of the trade in a special fun section for aspiring detectives.

❑ **Nate the Great and the Monster Mess**: Nate loves his mother's deliciously spooky Monster Cookies, but the recipe has vanished! This is one case Nate and his growling stomach can't afford to lose.

❑ **Nate the Great, San Francisco Detective**: Nate visits his cousin Olivia Sharp in the big city, but it's no vacation. Can he find a lost joke book in time to save the world?

❑ **Nate the Great and the Big Sniff**: Nate depends on his dog, Sludge, to help him solve all his cases. But Nate is on his own this time, because Sludge has disappeared! Can Nate solve the case and recover his canine buddy?

❑ **Nate the Great on the Owl Express**: Nate boards a train to guard Hoot, his cousin Olivia Sharp's pet owl. Then Hoot vanishes! Can Nate find out *whooo* took the feathered creature?